h₂o

Just add water!

Moon Spell

D1585828

C 03 0222630

Read other titles in the series

h_2O

Just add
water!

1 No Ordinary Girl

2 Living With Secrets

3 Fishy Business

4 A Sleepover Tail

5 Sequins for Sea Queens

6 First Crush

Adapted by Sue Behrent

SIMON AND SCHUSTER

SIMON AND SCHUSTER

First published in Great Britain in 2010 by Simon & Schuster UK Ltd,
1st Floor, 222 Gray's Inn Road, London WC1X 8HB
A CBS Company
Originally published in Australia in 2007 by Parragon
Licenced by ZDF Enterprises GmbH, Mainz
© A JMSP Programme in association with FFC, PFTC, Network 10, ZDF
German Television Network and ZDF Enterprises GmbH
© 2010 Viacom International Inc. All Rights Reserved. Nickelodeon, Splat
and all related titles, logos and characters are trademarks of Viacom
International Inc.

A CIP catalogue record for this book is available from the British Library

ISBN 978-1-84738-774-5

10 9 8 7 6 5 4 3 2 1

Printed by CPI Cox & Wyman, Reading, Berkshire RG1 8EX

Chapter 1

Emma, clipboard in hand, glided through from the kitchen into the lounge room and checked her list again. *The stereo is hooked up over here – check. I have the fairy lights strung up over there – check. The balloons... what's this?*

A solitary balloon had come away from a bunch that had been tied festively to a light fixture and now lay untidily on the floor. *What's this doing on the ground?* Emma thought to herself. She looked over her list once more. No, she had not authorized stray balloons to bounce messily around the room!

She picked up the offending balloon and shook it in the direction of her younger brother, Elliot.

"Make sure you tie them *tight*," Emma ordered. "It *has* to be a double knot."

Elliot looked up at her from where he sat

decorating the stairway handrails, rolled his eyes and went back to tying more balloons.

I know Em wants this to be the best party ever, but I wish she had more of the party spirit! he thought as he tried unsuccessfully to tie a double knot in the balloon he was stringing to the railing.

"That's wrong," Emma suddenly barked in Elliot's ear, causing him to jump. "We can't have black balloons!"

"Sorry," Elliot mumbled apologetically. The black ones had been all he could find in the kitchen drawers and there hadn't been time to go out and get more from the shops.

When 'Operation Emma' swings into action, no one is safe! Elliot thought cheekily.

"It's a party, Elliot," said Emma as she eyed the black balloons distastefully. "Happy, cheerful – *these* are your watchwords!"

Emma lowered her voice as they heard footsteps outside on the veranda and looked through the open front door to see Cleo and

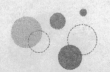
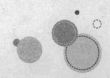

2

Rikki carefully wiping their feet on the front door mat.

"Hey!" they both called out to her as the two girls wandered into the hallway... and stopped suddenly in their tracks.

"Welcome to my gothic world," Rikki announced, flinging her arms out dramatically as she caught sight of the black balloons strung up along the staircase.

"That's not funny," said Emma irritably. "It's my dad's birthday, it's an important night!"

Am I the only one taking this seriously? Emma thought with frustration. *First the black balloons and now my friends are laughing at me and... and...*

Cleo nudged Rikki and nodded towards Emma, who with her clenched jaw and staring eyes, appeared to be about to burst!

"I don't think she's in the mood for your jokes," Cleo whispered discreetly.

Rikki nodded in agreement. Cleo knew Emma better than she did and if Cleo was

3

warning her against making any more jokes then Rikki figured the safest option was to listen to that advice. Maybe she could even try to put Emma at ease a bit.

"I can't believe you've organized this whole thing by yourself," she said, hurriedly changing the subject. "It's very, um… *efficient*," Rikki finished, pleased that she'd thought of the most perfect compliment for Emma. In the relatively short time she'd known Emma, she'd quickly realized that her new friend valued efficiency above almost everything else. *With organization coming a close second of course*, Rikki thought to herself.

Emma, happy to have *someone* acknowledge her hard work, relaxed her shoulders a little and led her friends into the kitchen.

"Have I told you about the seafood?" she asked, suddenly swinging around on Cleo.

Cleo threw up her hands defensively, palms out, in an effort to settle Emma's mounting panic.

"Only 25 times," she replied soothingly as

4

she threw Rikki another warning glance.

Rikki better behave herself, Cleo thought anxiously, *Emma is right on the edge with trying to organize this party!!*

Emma, however, was barely listening. She'd spied a small puddle of spilt dipping sauce on the kitchen bench and was scrubbing furiously to remove it.

"Tell your dad it needs to be *fresh* and it has to be his *best* stuff," said Emma, grunting with effort. "We need to have it here by seven forty-five," she added, looking up at Cleo and smiling broadly as she surveyed the now spotless bench.

"Okay," Cleo replied.

"You'd better write that down," said Emma as she opened a kitchen drawer and pulled out a pen.

Cleo looked around for a piece of scrap paper but all of the bench tops and the kitchen table itself were immaculate. There wasn't a single newspaper, invoice book or any other of the bits and pieces of paper that usually

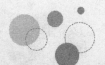

5

littered the tabletops in her own home. In fact, all of the surfaces in Emma's kitchen looked so thoroughly polished that Cleo thought any stray paper that did happen to land there would instantly slip off.

Failing to find anything else to write on, she took the pen Emma offered and wrote '7.45' on her hand instead. *If writing this down makes Emma feel a little less stressed about the seafood platters, then that's what I'll do*, she thought to herself, although even Cleo had to admit that Emma was acting a little bossily, even by her standards.

Rikki eyed Emma narrowly.

"You seem a bit… *tense*," she suggested.

"I'm *not* tense," Emma responded a bit too quickly, before grinning broadly at Rikki to show her just how *un*-tense she was. Although from where Rikki stood, it looked much more like Emma was simply baring her teeth!

"But you're… you're grinding your teeth," Rikki grimaced, pointing to her own mouth.

"It's called a *smile*, Rikki," said Emma

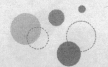
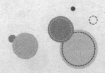

6

firmly before being distracted by Elliot walking through the kitchen clutching another bunch of balloons. "*Elliot*, don't do just yellow and black, get some other colours," she barked.

Elliot stopped and stared at his sister.

All morning it's been 'Elliot do this' and 'Elliot do that'! According to Emma I can't do anything right! If I didn't know how much this meant to her, I'd be out of here and down the beach practising my surfing!

But aloud, Elliot just let out a long-suffering sigh. "All right, *all right*. Sheesh!" he groaned as he started to edge around his sister on his way back through to the lounge.

"If you want something done *right*," Emma started to say, before – *PING* – Elliot bounced a balloon off her face as he passed her. She ignored it and went on to say, "…you've got to do it yourself."

Emma stood with her hands on her hips and glared at her friends, daring them to laugh at what had just happened.

But Rikki and Cleo glanced quickly at each

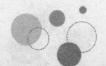

7

other and suppressed their giggles. This wasn't the time to wind Emma up any further; she was already like a coiled spring.

Seeing that the girls had chosen to be sensible, Emma proceeded to get down to business. There was work to do! She unclipped two pieces of paper from her clipboard and handed one each to Cleo and Rikki.

"The night's itinerary," she said, before reading aloud from her own copy of the list. "Okay, we'll do meet and greet from eight to eight-forty, dad arrives at eight-fifty."

"And what if he doesn't?" asked Cleo innocently.

"It's squash night; he's as regular as clockwork," said Emma, rolling her eyes as if to say it was obvious that her dad *would* be home as scheduled, because that is what she, Emma, had on the itinerary!

She raised her eyebrows at her two friends, as if challenging them to ask any more questions. When Cleo and Rikki just shook them meekly, Emma gave a satisfied *hmph*, and

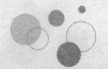
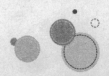

8

continued to read from her itinerary.

"We'll have surprise and congratulations until nine p.m. and refreshments whilst Elliot plays oboe until nine-ten." She looked up at Cleo and Rikki, who seconds before had been staring at her with alarm, to see their heads bent studiously over their itineraries.

Satisfied that they were finally taking the preparations seriously, Emma went on.

"At nine-forty the seafood will be served."

Rikki examined her itinerary for a moment.

"You've got a gap here between nine-ten and nine-forty," she said, pointing at her piece of paper.

"That's when I read my speech," said Emma proudly. "I've timed it at twenty-six minutes and forty-five seconds approximately, leaving a little over three minutes for applause and congratulations."

Rikki blinked rapidly. *Uh, is it just me or is this really weird?!* she thought to herself. *Will Emma crack if the congratulations go over their*

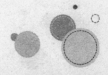

9

allotted three minutes? And a 27 minute speech? Oh I don't know about this...

"Sounds more like a battle plan than a party," said Rikki, trying to lighten the tone.

But Emma was in no mood to listen to Rikki's advice, well-meaning or otherwise. Ignoring her, she cleared her throat and said, "I need to test out my speech."

Rikki groaned. She didn't know how much more of all this she could stand! It was a beautiful day outside and here they were, cooped up inside with Little Miss Bossy giving orders and about to embark on the longest birthday speech known to humankind!

She scuttled around the breakfast bar, pulled up a stool and plonked herself down. If she was going to have to listen to the speech in its entirety, she might as well make herself comfortable!

Cleo's eyes glazed over at the thought of having to concentrate for a whole 26 minutes. *It's not like I'm not interested*, she thought to herself, as she watched Emma shuffle her

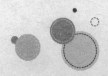

10

papers into order, *but that's a long time for anyone to sit still. I wonder what I should wear tonight...* Cleo drifted off.

"Dear dad," Emma began, "Happy birthday to the most magnificent, debonair, generous, kind dad in the entire world. Where do I start? At the beginning, of course. Day one; I'm born."

Emma looked up from her speech; both Cleo and Rikki seemed to be hanging on her every word!

... perhaps that green dress, the one with the beading. I should really remember to ask Emma and Rikki what they're wearing; we don't want to all turn up in similar outfits! What a disaster that'd be! Cleo mused to herself.

... I can't ever in a million years imagine organizing a surprise party for my dad, pondered Rikki. *And even if I could, I would* never *say any of that rubbish!*

Emma smiled happily, confident that she had her friends' full attention, and continued reading with even more animation.

"The first person I laid eyes on was *you*; father and daughter smile, it was love at first sight."

"That's beautiful," chimed in Cleo.

"Uhhhh," said Rikki wracking her brain for an appropriate comment. "Maybe it needs some editing?" she finally suggested.

Emma ran her eye down the speech. *Editing?* she thought wonderingly. "You think?" she added aloud.

"Oh, it's just a thought," Rikki replied hastily.

Cleo stretched and yawned.

"I've got to go, I've got to work at two," she said and seeing that Emma had something she desperately wanted to say, Cleo quickly added, "But I'm going home first to let dad know what time he's to deliver the seafood platter *and* I'll be back here in plenty of time for the meet and greet at…" Cleo stopped and consulted her itinerary, "… at eight."

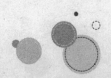

12

Emma's mouth snapped shut and she nodded briskly, satisfied that Cleo would do what she said she'd do.

"Well, all that seems okay," she said, seeing Cleo to the door. "We'll see you later then."

"Yep, later," said Cleo, giving them both a friendly wave and running down the steps and out through the front gate.

Emma walked back into the kitchen and picked up her speech.

"I'll read through the whole thing for you and *you* tell *me* where you think it needs some editing," Emma said sarcastically to Rikki.

Oh! I should've kept my big mouth shut! thought Rikki miserably.

"Dear dad," Emma began all over again, careful to pronounce every word and syllable correctly. "Happy birthday to the most magnificent, debonair, generous…"

NOOOOOOOOOOOO! Rikki screamed inside.

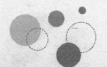

13

Chapter 2

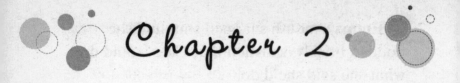

Later that afternoon, Cleo stood behind the counter of the food cart at the marine park. There had been plenty of people about and she'd been busy, but now as the afternoon wore on, the crowds had thinned and Cleo was taking advantage of the lull to daydream about the outfit she planned on wearing to Emma's dad's party.

I forgot to ask Emma and Rikki what they're wearing tonight, Cleo thought as she mentally kicked herself. *I knew I would! But I guess it's probably for the best; I don't want Emma to stress about that as well as everything else she has to think about. I'll text them later...*

Something out of the corner of her eye caught Cleo's attention. An old woman, brightly dressed in various shades of blue, appeared to be watching her. Half-ducked

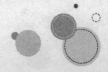

14

down behind some bushes, the woman peered this way and that, checking that the coast was clear before bursting out of the foliage and bustling along the path towards Cleo.

It wasn't until she got closer that Cleo realized she knew the woman. She'd met her a month or more ago, when she'd first started working at the marine park. The woman had come backstage and acted really mysteriously, saying odd stuff like how important it was for her to keep dry and how the salt water stings when it splashes into your eyes, but not when you're swimming underwater!

I hope she's not going to cause trouble, thought Cleo nervously, although the determined way the woman was approaching her did nothing to dispel her anxiety.

The woman trotted up to the food stand, gave one last look around and leaned forward conspiratorially.

"I've come to warn you," she said in hushed tones.

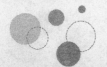

"Warn me about what?" asked Cleo, alarm bells ringing in her head, but trying to be polite. But if the woman sensed that Cleo was nervous or not taking her seriously, she didn't show it.

"Don't *ever* talk to sea perch, you can't trust those fish," she continued seriously, frowning slightly at the thought of the dishonest sea creatures.

Cleo looked her up and down; she saw now that the woman was dressed in layers of a light blue-green gauzy fabric that billowed around her with every gust of warm wind. It looked to Cleo as if the woman was being borne along by a series of breaking waves! *That must've been why I thought she looked so strange when she was coming towards me*, Cleo thought to herself, pleased that she'd been able to pinpoint what it was about the woman that had made her feel uneasy. *Look at those earrings; they're little silver seahorses!*

Aloud Cleo asked, "*Why* would I talk to fish?"

The woman closed her eyes and concentrated

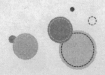

16

for a second before opening them again.

"Listen carefully, it's very important. You must *not* look at the moon's *eye*," she said, mysteriously drawing out the word 'eye' to give it an extra sense of importance.

"The moon's...?" asked Cleo, not understanding anything the woman was trying to tell her.

"The *full* moon. It's dangerous," the woman said earnestly. "Do not look at it *or* its reflection."

Cleo nodded. Although she wasn't *exactly* frightened by the woman it seemed like a smart move to just nod and agree with everything she said.

"And when it's *out*, do not touch water... *whatever you do*," the woman went on, sighing slightly as she said the last three words.

"But..." Cleo was just about to ask when she heard someone call her name.

"Hi, Cleo!" Rikki and Emma approached the food stand, smiling and looking relaxed.

17

In fact Emma looked calmer than Cleo had seen her for a while.

She just needed to get out of that house and get her mind off the preparations! Cleo thought, happy to see Emma, her arms full of parcels, chatting animatedly to Rikki.

Cleo glanced around to see where the old woman had got to, but she'd disappeared... *just like last time we met!* she thought, baffled.

"Did you see *that*?" Cleo asked as Rikki and Emma reached the food stand.

Both girls looked at her questioningly.

"See what?" asked Rikki.

"That old woman, she was standing just there," Cleo replied, pointing to the place where the woman had been leaning.

"*What* old woman?" Rikki asked again.

Now it was Cleo's turn to act mysterious. She looked over her shoulder to check that there was no one within earshot and then leaned closer to the two girls.

18

"She *knows* about us. She said something about the full moon being dangerous," Cleo hissed.

Rikki and Emma looked around. There was no one around to see and there certainly hadn't been anyone talking to Cleo when they'd spied the food stand from way down the path.

"I didn't see anyone," said Emma matter-of-factly.

"Me neither," added Rikki with a shrug of her shoulders.

Cleo eyed them both doubtfully. How could they have *not* seen the old woman? She'd been right there!

"She told me not to talk to sea perch and something about reflections," she continued persistently, trying to remember everything the woman had told her; "... and beware the full moon."

Rikki wondered if Cleo kept horror comics behind the counter for when there were no customers around to serve. *Maybe that's where*

19

she's getting these odd ideas, she thought, raising her eyebrows slightly in surprise. Cleo was the last person she would have thought of to make up those sorts of stories.

"Sounds like she'd had a bit too much sun," Rikki said sensibly, hoping to put an end to Cleo's fantasies.

But Cleo shook her head; she *knew* that wasn't all there was to it.

"There's *something* different about her," she said thoughtfully, more to herself than the others.

Emma and Rikki exchanged glances; maybe it was *Cleo* who had had a bit too much sun!

Emma knew exactly what would cheer Cleo out of her weird mood.

What she needs is a good dose of retail revelation and I have just the thing, Emma thought happily, putting her parcels on the counter and locating the one she'd been thinking of.

"But not as different as *these*," she cried,

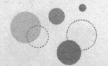
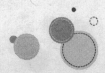

20

presenting with a flourish the most beautiful pair of shoes any of them had seen for a long time! "*Gorgeous* aren't they?"

Cleo's eyes lit up at the sight of them, the old woman already forgotten.

"They're *really* nice," she cooed, delighted that her friend had managed to find something so fabulous. They were a light, coral-pink suede complete with a beautiful purple diamante on the toe, which caught the sun and sent glittery reflections spinning around the food stand.

All three girls stood transfixed by the beauty of the shoes, only to be jolted out of their daze by the sound of someone walking past.

"Hey, Em," called Byron, raising a hand in greeting.

Emma felt her cheeks redden and hastily put the shoes back in their box.

"Oh, hey Byron," she replied as casually as she could, flicking her hair off one shoulder and throwing him a smile.

"See you tonight," he smiled back, to which

21

Emma simply nodded in reply. Neither Byron nor even Rikki or Cleo could've guessed that Emma had posted Byron's invitation personally. The rest she'd simply given to her mother to send. But not Byron's; she'd wanted to make *extra* sure his arrived safely. *And as I always say*, Emma mused to herself, *if you want something done…*

Suddenly she heard that someone was snickering at her. Strike that, it was *two* people!

Emma took one last look at Byron walking off towards the display pool and turned back to her friends.

To her great embarrassment, she saw Rikki exaggeratedly flicking her hair off her shoulders and pouting as Cleo squealed with laughter.

"What's all *this* about?" asked Rikki, laughing kind-heartedly as she flicked her hair once more for emphasis.

Emma smirked. They'd caught her flirting and now they were going to make her *pay*!

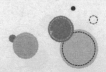

22

"Don't be stupid," she grinned in reply. "There's nothing going on with Byron. Forget it!"

But the half-hearted denial just made Rikki and Cleo scream with laughter all over again.

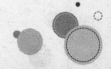

Chapter 3

Emma's mum paced anxiously around the house, looking approvingly at the balloons and streamers Emma and Elliot had used to decorate the rooms for the party.

"I feel a bit *guilty* just hanging around," she said to Emma who had just walked into the room.

"Thanks Mum, but… I really want to do this on my own," said Emma looking around happily at what they'd accomplished. She felt really pleased with herself and with Elliot too; the party rooms looked fantastic!

"I'm *so* proud of you, sweetheart, and I know your dad is too," said her mum, smiling warmly at her daughter. "And I think tonight's party is going to be one that we're going to remember for a very, *very* long time."

She flung her arm around Emma's shoulders and gave her daughter a big hug. She was so proud of her. Well, not only Emma, but of her whole family. *How many other mums have kids who would put in this kind of work organizing a surprise party for their father*, she thought. *I really do have the perfect family.*

It was five minutes to eight o'clock and the guests were beginning to arrive in precise accordance with Emma's itinerary.

"This is going to be *so* great," said Emma enthusiastically to Cleo and Rikki as they stood in line at the door receiving guests and taking jackets to put in the spare room. She was already much calmer now that the party had started at the correct time, and very relieved to know that there wouldn't be any stragglers arriving as her dad got home – that would blow the whole surprise!

Cleo and Rikki smiled. It was good to see that Emma was going to get the chance to have a good time at the party she'd spent so much time and effort organizing. Nothing would have been worse than seeing her stuck in the kitchen

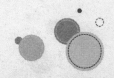

25

all night stressing about the arrangements! They knew from experience that less stress for Emma meant less stress for them!

Cleo's dad had arrived earlier, right on the dot of 7.45 p.m. – as repeatedly instructed to by Cleo – with the seafood platters. Emma had whisked them away to the upstairs bathroom where they were now cooling on ice in the bathtub.

So far, so good, thought Cleo happily, although something from earlier that afternoon still niggled in the back of her mind.

"I can't stop thinking about what that old woman said," Cleo whispered to Rikki between polite smiles as they both greeted the next guests coming through the door. "Beware the full moon and all that."

Rikki took another guest's coat and waved the woman airily into the party room – Cleo seemed to know most of the people Emma had invited, but Rikki just had to make do with smiling warmly as they arrived and pointing them towards the party without calling

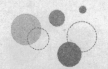

26

them by name. There was plenty of time for introductions later in the night.

"We're mermaids, *not* werewolves," Rikki whispered back before taking the latest coat into the spare room and flinging it onto the bed with the others.

She jostled back to her place by the door just in time to see one of the most sour-faced old biddies she had ever seen in her life waltz through the door. "Aunt Thea!" She heard Emma exclaim. "So glad you could come!"

Aunt Thea was pushing an elderly lady in a wheelchair and Emma bent down and gave the woman a warm hug.

"Hi Grandma, you look gorgeous tonight," Emma said cheerily.

"So do you, sweetheart," her grandma replied, pinching Emma's cheek kindly while looking excitedly around the party and catching sight of her daughter-in-law. She gave her a wave and Emma's mum waved back and rushed over to greet her.

Aunt Thea, meanwhile, gave Cleo and Rikki

27

an appraising glance up and down. Her sour reaction suggested that she didn't like the look of what she saw at all! She wrinkled her nose slightly with distaste, but was quickly distracted by the arrival of Emma's mum, who led both Aunt Thea and Grandma off in the direction of the comfiest sofa in the lounge room.

The next person through the door was an extremely handsome middle-aged man with a much younger, slightly *orange*-tinged woman attached to his arm.

"Doctor Bennett, it's *great* you could come," said Emma charmingly. As soon as she heard Emma say the man's name, Rikki quickly put the pieces together in her head and realized that the man standing in front of her must have been Zane Bennett's dad. *But who's that gold-digger he's with*? she thought.

"I don't believe you've met Candy," smiled Dr Bennett. And with his arm already draped across the shoulders of the young woman, he drew her forward to be introduced.

Emma leaned in and held out her hand.

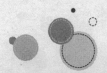

28

"Hi Candy, *love* your dress," said Emma, shaking Candy's hand and admiring her dress all in one movement.

"You're sweet," giggled Candy in reply.

Rikki sucked in her cheeks to check the laughter she felt mounting in her chest. *That voice! She sounds like a cartoon character*, she thought, *and that* orange *skin… that's straight out of a tanning bottle for sure. What an airhead!*

But she heard Emma continue smoothly, "I'm so pleased all Dad's business associates are coming tonight."

It's like she didn't even hear Candy's piercing tone, thought Rikki, baffled. She had to hand it to Emma, she was handling the guests like a pro.

Dr Bennett and Candy drifted off to join the other guests as Miriam and Zane breezed in after them.

Emma's mum had insisted that Emma invite the pair, even though she'd rather not have. But as her mum had pointed out, both Miriam

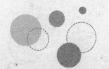
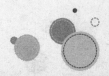

and Zane's parents were old friends of the family and it would have been poor form to leave them off the guest list.

"The place looks great," said Zane genuinely, smiling at the three girls as he sauntered in. Rikki bristled. She didn't trust Zane or Miriam as far as she could throw them. Every time she'd been forced to have anything to do with either of them, things had ended badly, and she didn't expect tonight to be an exception to the rule. But then she couldn't exactly kick them out of her friend's party, however much she would have liked to.

So I'll just have to keep my eyes peeled for when they start making a nuisance of themselves. And when they do... I'll be there with bells on! Rikki thought maliciously. *It just won't do to have them spoil the party after Emma's put so much work into it.*

"Thanks, Zane," said Emma, keeping her voice neutral but looking daggers at Miriam, who was doing a rather impressive job of sneering at three things at once: the decorations, Emma's choice of music and all

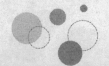
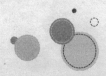

30

three of the girls' outfits.

Rikki was still staring suspiciously after Miriam and Zane when Lewis ambled in.

"*Lewis*, right on time," Emma exclaimed delightedly when she saw him.

"Yes, well, I'm a sucker for parties," replied Lewis, touched by the genuine welcome in Emma's voice.

"*Good*!" said Emma, suddenly becoming all business-like again. "I need you to stand on door duty whilst I get some drinks."

Lewis stood with his mouth agape, watching as first Emma, followed closely by Cleo and Rikki, flashed him their brightest smiles and then dashed off towards the kitchen, leaving him standing alone at the door looking helplessly at their retreating backs.

Suddenly he heard a cough behind him and he spun around.

"Welcome!" Lewis said, smiling broadly, taking the next guest's jacket.

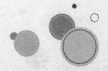

31

Chapter 4

Emma hustled into the kitchen. She'd set up the finger-food and pre-poured most of the drinks before the guests had arrived so all she had to do was pick up a serving tray and circulate.

Shall I take the canapés or the drinks out first? she wondered, before spotting the punch bowl. *Oh, maybe I should take the punch out first and put it on the coffee table and then people can help themselves.*

But as Emma looked at the punch bowl something strange caught her eye. Outside, the full moon had suddenly appeared from behind a cloud and its reflection filled the whole punch bowl – almost as if it was completely filled up with *moon* not punch!

Emma stood mesmerized by the beauty of it. She couldn't look away.

A strange feeling suddenly washed over

Emma. She felt a weird tingling sensation in her legs, like pins and needles, which slowly creaped up her body until it felt as if her head was full of cotton balls – all fluffy and light. Emma raised her hands to her face – it was ice cold! *What's the matter with me?* thought Emma, *I hope I'm not getting sick or something.* But just as suddenly as this thought had occurred to her, it slipped away again. Her brain was whizzing and whirring with one thought replacing another so quickly that nothing was making sense any more! Emma felt dizzy, her vision became clouded and when it cleared slightly she could see what looked like rainbow-coloured auras around everything. A peculiar sparkly noise sounded in her ears, as if someone right beside her had just opened a can of fizzy drink.

That's so amazing, she thought to herself. *The moon is so incredibly beautiful and… exquisite! And talking of exquisite, how good is this party? Everyone's really pulled together and done such a fantastic job…*

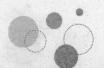

33

Emma's mum came into the kitchen and busied herself in the fridge.

"Your grandma is having such a lovely time, Em. I haven't seen her looking so well in ages, didn't you think so?" she asked over her shoulder.

Emma stood stiffly, staring out of the window into the very depths of the bright, shining moon.

When she didn't get a reply, Emma's mum pulled her head out from the back of the fridge. "Did you hear me, Emma? I said your Grandma hasn't looked so... Em? *Em?* Are you all right?"

Emma started out of her hypnotic state and smiled serenely at her mother.

"Hmmm," she said dreamily and picked up a tray of spring rolls.

I haven't eaten anything for ages*! I might just have a little nibble now*, thought Emma, eyeing the tray of food hungrily.

I think I'll try... Emma's finger hovered over

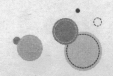

34

the food, *eeny, meeny… this one!*

She bit into one of the delicious snacks. *Mmmmmm, that's good!* she thought as she finished off the spring roll and reached for another one.

Emma swept into the lounge room still chomping on the spring rolls and wandered up to Miriam, Zane and Candy who stood together talking.

"Hey Emma, great party," said Zane politely.

But Emma, mouth full of food, ignored him and thrust the plate at Miriam temptingly.

Miriam swept an assessing eye over the snacks.

There must be a thousand empty calories in those spring rolls, she thought, shrinking back from the plate. It seemed to Emma as if Miriam was worried the calories would jump right off the platter on to her waist!

"I think you'd like *this* one," said Emma conspiratorially, offering Miriam the half-eaten spring roll she held in her hand.

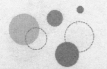

35

"Uh, *gross*," replied Miriam, wrinkling up her nose and backing even further away from Emma and the plate of food.

Emma shrugged her shoulders and turned her attention to Candy.

"You look *way* too young to be Zane's father's girlfriend," she said conversationally.

Zane snorted and choked on this drink, which in turn brought on a fit of coughing.

Candy stood and stared at Emma for a moment, too stunned to speak.

"*I beg your pardon*?" she asked finally from between clenched teeth.

"I guess you're just after the money though," Emma replied happily, giving Candy a friendly squeeze on the arm before turning away to offer the food elsewhere.

Zane wiped the tears from his eyes as he struggled to keep from bursting into peals of laughter.

I wonder what's got into Emma? he thought. *This isn't like her at all! But whatever it is, I like*

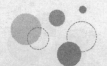
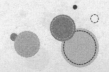

36

it!

From across the room Rikki heard raised voices, saw that things weren't going well and hustled over just in time to hear Emma's final comment.

"What's *wrong* with you?" she hissed the second she could get Emma alone.

"Nothing's *wrong* with me, Rikki-baby, I feel fantastic," replied Emma, pinching Rikki's cheeks.

Rikki-baby?! Rikki thought, *did Emma, of all people, just refer to me as Rikki-baby?!* She couldn't believe what she was hearing!

From over Rikki's shoulder, Emma suddenly spied someone who needed her help!

Oh, Doctor Bennett looks starving! she thought. *I better get some food over there right away, it's an 'emergency'.*

Emma giggled at her own joke as she weaved her way to Doctor Bennett's side. Rikki followed close behind.

Doctor Bennett selected a spring roll from

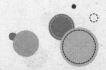

37

the tray Emma was offering and took a bite.

"I wish I had a daughter who went to all this trouble for me," he said pleasantly.

Emma smiled and peered at him closely; something else had caught her attention.

"You've got a lot of hair growing out of your nose there, Harrison," she said teasingly. "It's a real forest."

Rikki inhaled sharply. *Something's not right here!* she thought, grabbing Emma by the arm and whirling her away from the doctor before he had time to react.

"We were just on our way to the bathroom," she smiled apologetically. "See you later," she added before taking Emma firmly by the shoulders and marching her towards the kitchen.

Aunt Thea, who'd been standing behind Doctor Bennett, leaned around him to stare after her niece.

How rude! she thought, shocked by Emma's impolite behaviour. *I'll have to talk to my*

38

brother about the way he's raising his children.

Aunt Thea gave Doctor Bennett a rueful look. *As long as he understands that kind of behaviour isn't tolerated in my family I'll… oh, Emma's right, he* does *have rather hairy nostrils.*

Rikki steered Emma through the guests and had almost got her to the kitchen and safety when Emma twisted free and grabbed her cousin's drink.

She looked at the bottle of water for a moment.

What a shame! Emma thought to herself, pressing her eye up to the glass and peeping in. *All those poor bubbles popping in there. Fizzing away for what? They're only going to get gulped down by Harriet. It hardly seems worth it! I need to liberate these bubbles, save them from Harriet's tummy!*

The thoughts whizzed around Emma's brain as she upended the bottle and tipped the water out onto the floor.

"I *love* the look of water," she sighed, captivated by the way the water collected on the floor. *Look! There goes some under the bench and there's some running under the sofa; no one is going to able to drink that! Oh and that bit is making a little pool… like the moon pool on Mako Island.*

A hush descended over the party. Emma's grandma looked on, her mouth a wide 'O' shape of dismay. In the corner, Zane sniggered. Even though he was far from being a prude, he had to admit that Emma may've gone a little too far even for him.

Suddenly Cleo jumped to Emma's side and took her arm.

"She's over-tired," she began explaining to the entire room, looking around pleadingly at the guests and thinking quickly on her feet. "She's been working *really* hard to get this party right. I'll take her outside for some fresh air."

Rikki and Cleo glanced at each other questioningly; neither of them had a clue what

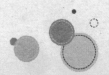

40

was going on with Emma but they knew they had to get her out of the party and quick!

But Emma wasn't quite ready to leave the party she'd worked so hard to put on!

Aunt Thea and Grandma were on the sofa talking about Emma and darting looks over their shoulders.

"What on earth has got into Emma?" asked Grandma.

"I don't know but I'll be speaking to Neil after the party. The girl's out of control! Did you hear the way she spoke to the doctor? It was disgraceful, the…"

"Aunt Thea!" called Emma loudly from the kitchen doorway, rudely interrupting their conversation.

Her Aunt looked up to see Emma grinning at her.

The guests stopped talking and craned their necks to see what was going to happen next. Emma wasn't supposed to be part of the entertainment, but she was turning out to be

41

the main attraction!

"Your tartan skirt!" said Emma mischievously. "Did you steal our *picnic rug*?"

Eventually, after much urging and coaxing, Cleo managed to get Emma safely outside. She thought the night air would perhaps do her friend some good – clear her thoughts a bit. Thankfully, no one had followed them out, so they were free to walk together unhurriedly until they arrived at the sun-loungers that Emma had placed strategically around the in-ground swimming pool. The lights were on in the pool and the strange light it threw off reflected playfully on the girls' faces.

They sat quietly without speaking for a minute, both lost in their own thoughts.

I don't know what's wrong with Emma this evening, thought Cleo, worriedly. *For the last couple of weeks all she's been talking about is her dad's birthday and how important it is to her to have everything exactly right. And now it seems as if she's trying to wreck the whole thing!*

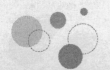
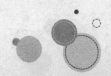

42

Cleo knew it was her duty as Emma's best friend to talk to her about how she was behaving but she didn't know where to start. In fact, Cleo was actually dreading it!

I'm too shy to talk to her about her bad manners, Cleo squirmed with embarrassment at the thought of it. *But if I don't... who will?*

Bracing herself for what she knew she had to say, Cleo had barely opened her mouth to begin when Emma jumped in first.

"Have you noticed how *weird* people look?" she suddenly said with a laugh. "Their legs just don't *look* right."

Startled, Cleo glanced over at Emma to see her lying back in the sun-lounger with her arms dangling over the sides as if everything was right with the world.

She's acting like that was an absolutely normal thing to say! thought Cleo, shocked at how strange Emma was behaving. But Emma simply took Cleo's silence as a sign of agreement and continued.

"Now take fish," she added thoughtfully.

43

"They're *sensibly* designed."

"Can I get you something?" Cleo asked quickly, looking for some kind of distraction and hoping to steer Emma's thoughts away from fish towards something more normal. She didn't like where the conversation was going at all.

Emma looked over at her in surprise and thought for a minute.

"I'd *love* a cheese sandwich on rye bread with sardines," she said enthusiastically.

Cleo nodded her head and got up to go inside and make the sandwich. *Maybe once Emma eats something... maybe then she'll feel normal again*, she thought anxiously.

"Y'know, *actually...*" said Emma, stopping Cleo with a wave of her hand, "forget the cheese and the bread, just bring me the sardines."

"*O-kay*," replied Cleo, pretending that someone eating sardines straight out of the can was the most normal thing in the world. *For a cat perhaps!* she thought glumly to herself.

44

She gave Emma another concerned look. "Don't go away, okay? I'll be right back."

Emma beamed back at her and nodded her head. "I'll stay right here," she said happily, leaning her head back on the sun-lounger and closing her eyes peacefully.

Casting one last look around the garden to reassure herself that Emma would be safe while she was away, Cleo went inside, closing the door behind her. She didn't want any guests going outside and disturbing Emma.

With any luck, Emma might fall asleep for a while and wake up feeling better! Cleo thought hopefully.

Even with her eyes shut, Emma knew that the moon had come out from behind the clouds again.

It's like when someone shines a torch in your face or puts the light on in your room when you're asleep… you always *know. Maybe my eyelids are thinner than I think!* Emma's eyes snapped open and she stared up into the brilliant white lunar light.

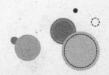

45

How beautiful and ancient it seems...

Random thoughts began to swirl around Emma's brain. They were like memories, but they weren't *her* memories. In her mind's eye she could see three mermaids darting through the water, but when the vision sharpened slightly, she realized it wasn't Cleo, Rikki and her – these were strangers, girls she'd never seen before! Their hair was cut very short, in an almost masculine style, and they wore necklaces of shiny stones. It was like watching a movie inside her head or a dream, even though she was obviously awake and in her back yard.

In her mind the girls turned around and saw her, smiled sweetly and beckoned for her to follow them.

Emma got to her feet and, still hypnotized by the moon's dazzling luminescence, padded across the deck and down to the dock that looked out onto the canal at the back of the house.

She stared into the cool, calm water.

The moon's reflection in the water looks like

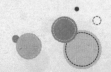

46

a silver path... a silver path I could follow until I reach the most wondrous place on earth. Or should I say the Universe! I know those girls would be waiting for me there. Emma smiled to herself as she slowly bent down, slipped off her beautiful new shoes and dived smoothly into the water.

Within seconds she felt the now familiar tingling in her legs, like tiny bubbles were popping against them, and with a flap of her mermaid's tail, Emma had disappeared beneath the water.

Chapter 5

Mr Gilbert was tired after his squash game, but he knew that his wife would be making something special for this birthday dinner and he was hungry. Not only that, but he was looking forward to spending another birthday with his family. *Elliot and Emma always get so excited about my birthday*, he thought to himself happily. *It's almost as if they enjoy my birthday more than their own!* Walking down the driveway from his car, he realized that his thoughts all added up to the fact that he was happy to be home. So he was very surprised when he came to the front door and noticed that all the lights were out inside.

Slightly concerned, he fumbled for his keys in the dark, unlocked the door and dumped his squash gear just inside the entrance. *This really is quite strange*, he thought, *where is everyone?*

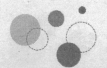
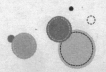

It's all dark in here and they would never forget my birthday.

Suddenly someone flicked the light switch and the room lit up.

"SURPRISE!!!" the guests yelled all together, jumping out from their hiding places.

Mr Gilbert laughed delightedly as Elliot and his wife ran up to give him a hug.

"Happy Birthday," said Mrs Gilbert excitedly.

"This *is* a surprise," he said happily, his arms around her. "Oh thank you, darling, this is more than I expected."

"Oh don't thank me, thank Emma. She did everything," replied Mrs Gilbert proudly.

Mr Gilbert looked around at the assembled guests, cheerfully nodding a greeting to his friends and business acquaintances before going over to kiss his mother.

"Where is that perfect daughter of mine?" he asked, looking around for Emma.

49

"I'll… I'll just go and find her for you," said Rikki who was standing nearby.

As Mr Gilbert circulated amongst his friends, Rikki rushed into the kitchen in search of Emma, only to find Cleo struggling to open a tin of sardines.

"I can *never* get these things to open," said Cleo, trying to tear off the lid of the can with the key still attached.

"You wanna eat *sardines*?" asked Rikki, astonished.

"*No*, they're for Emma," replied Cleo, horrified by the very thought of eating something as oily and smelly as sardines.

"Where *is* Emma?" asked Rikki slowly, sensing a problem. She didn't want to believe that Cleo had left Emma outside on her own, but she couldn't see another explanation.

"She's outside, where I left her," Cleo replied absently, still preoccupied with the can.

"By *herself* outside?" said Rikki worriedly.

The two girls looked at each other for a

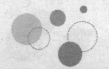
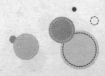

split-second before Cleo slipped the can into the pocket of her jacket and raced outside with Rikki right on her heels.

"She was right here on this sun-lounger when I went inside," wailed Cleo, looking around the now-empty deck.

"Yeah, well she's not here now," said Rikki pragmatically. She knew there was no sense in blaming Cleo for Emma disappearing. "She couldn't have gone far though, let's check out the dock and see if she's down there getting some air."

"Oh Rikki, I hope she's okay. She's been acting so strangely since the party started," said Cleo, her voice full of concern.

"Yeah I know," said Rikki grimly, leading the way down to the canal.

Emma powered swiftly through the water, leaving a wake of tiny silvery bubbles trailing behind her.

I've never felt so free... she thought to

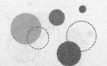
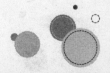

51

herself, feeling the currents softly caressing her skin and flowing through her hair. Every part of her was alive to the movements and sensations of the sea.

Sensing that she was nearing land, Emma slowed her passage and swam up to the surface, popping her head above the waves and peering around to assess her position. At that very moment, the moon peeped out from behind the clouds and illuminated the jagged outline of Mako Island.

Mako Island... Emma sighed. *This is where it all began... how could I have ever wished to go back to my old life? I'm a mermaid; it's who I am now. It is me.*

"They're Emma's new shoes," shouted Rikki as she ran down to the dock with Cleo.

The two girls sped over the remaining distance to where the shoes lay and Rikki picked them up to examine them.

They're dry; that's a good sign, she thought, relieved. *It means that she is aware enough of what she's doing to take her shoes off, not jump*

in fully clothed.

"There's something just not right about this," said Cleo suspiciously, gazing around the empty dock, before walking right to the edge and peering over into the inky blackness of the water.

"That's the understatement of the year," mumbled Rikki in reply.

All of sudden they heard footsteps slapping on the planks of the deck and the next minute they saw Lewis come trudging down the dock towards them.

"I've been looking *everywhere* for you guys,' he said, pleased to have found them at last, "Have you two seen Emma?"

"We found these," said Cleo, gesturing to Emma's shoes and then looking back seriously to Lewis. "And they're..."

"Are they Emma's?" Lewis asked.

Without warning, the dark clouds above them drifted apart, allowing the moon to shine brightly down on the dock with its full brilliance. Cleo and Rikki looked up at it, struck

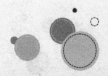

53

by how dazzlingly it glowed in the night sky.

It turns night into day... thought Cleo joyfully, completely entranced by the moon's radiance.

"*Cleo*? Are they Emma's?" Lewis repeated again more insistently, turning to face her as he spoke.

What's wrong with these two? Lewis thought to himself. *They look like they're... in a trance!*

Lewis reached up and clicked his fingers in front of Cleo's face.

Nothing.

He snapped his fingers in Rikki's face, only inches from her nose. "*Rikki*?" he said loudly.

Nothing.

Lewis turned back to Cleo and poked her in the cheek gently. "*Cleo*?"

No response. Interesting... it's like she's under a spell or something...

Lewis looked up at the moon and back at his two friends, who stared at it, seemingly

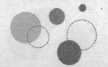
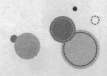

54

captivated by its beaming light.

Ahhh, so that's it, he thought as the full significance of what was happening suddenly dawned on him. *The moon is affecting them somehow. That's a new development in this ongoing mermaid saga!* Lewis smiled to himself. *And if they're spellbound... well, that means they don't know what's going on around them. And if that's the case then that means...*

Lewis turned to Rikki and laughed mischievously.

... it's payback time!

He raised his hand and reached over to give one of Rikki's pigtails a firm but gentle yank. *This is for all the times you've been sarcastic, demanding and generally unpleasant!*

At just that moment, the clouds scudded over the face of the moon, breaking its hold over Cleo and Rikki as its light faded from view.

Lewis's hand was already halfway to Rikki's head when she shot her own hand up and grabbed him tightly around the wrist. Her

reflexes were lightning fast.

"That would be a *big* mistake," said Rikki with a warning look.

Lewis wrenched his hand free from her grasp and looked from one girl to the other.

"I'm sorry, but you guys just went *extremely* weird when the moon came out," he explained, quickly wiping the smile off his face. *That was a very near thing*, he breathed silently with relief.

Cleo looked at Rikki in shock as she mentally recalled the events from the marine park earlier in the day.

"This is what the old woman meant," she said excitedly. "She was trying to warn us."

Rikki nodded her head in agreement, but Lewis was perplexed. This was the first he'd heard of any old woman. And more to the point, it was the first he'd heard of anyone else offering the girls advice. That was *his* job!

"What old woman?" he asked, not a little put out that no one had thought to mention any of this to him before now.

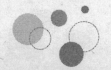
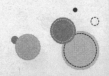

"That first night at the moon pool on Mako Island was a full moon as well," said Rikki, ignoring Lewis's question entirely.

Suddenly, the three of them heard splashing sounds from the canal and ran to the side of the dock to see what was in the water.

Emma stared up at them, smiling happily.

"You guys have *got to* come in," she said, delighted.

She tipped her head back and stared at the sky as she slowly and rhythmically moved her arms back and forth in the water.

"Mako Island is *amazing* at night," she sighed, gazing up at the star-encrusted sky and then looking back to her friends on the dock, her eyes wide as if she was enthralled by every single thing that came into her sight.

Lewis gulped. He'd never seen Emma act like this before. Was she flirting with him? Whatever she was doing, it made him feel uncomfortable.

"I've never seen anything like it," said

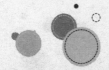

57

Emma, raising her eyebrows and holding Lewis's gaze.

Rikki had had enough. *This is getting out of control; we need to get her out of the water, dried and dressed and back inside!* she thought to herself. She could see how awkward Lewis was with the whole situation too, not to mention how embarrassed Emma would be when she got back to normal and found out how she'd behaved!

If she gets back to normal, she thought grimly.

"Lewis, pull her out, *now*," Rikki ordered.

Lewis took a step back from the side of the dock and stared at Rikki in amazement.

"*Me*? Why does it have to be me?" he asked, his voice rising an octave in annoyance.

"Well it's obvious *we* can't get wet," Rikki replied reasonably. "We could fall under the same moon spell and then you'd have to pull us *all* out."

Lewis shuddered at the thought of them all

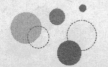
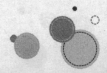

acting as full-on and weirdly as Emma. And then he imagined trying to wrestle three crazed mermaids out of the water at once.

"Come to Mako Island with me," Emma said enticingly, beckoning to them. "It's the most wonderful place. It's like an underwater wonderland."

Cleo and Rikki exchanged another fearful glance. This was getting stranger by the minute.

"Mmmm. We could live down there *forever*," Emma added alluringly.

Okay, now she's really creeping me out! thought Lewis desperately, taking a deep breath and mentally preparing himself. *This is going to take some skilled negotiating.*

"Emma, of *course* we'll come with you, you… you just take my hand and you can show me the way," he said as if he was talking to a naughty five-year-old, leaning towards her and holding out his hand.

Emma looked up at him doubtfully for a second, sensing a trap, before holding out her hand and clutching his. Suddenly she let out a

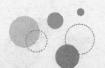

59

cheeky laugh and tugged him head over heels into the water.

Lewis didn't know what had happened. One minute he was standing on the dock, all warm and dry and now he was flailing in the black water. *I can't see a thing!* he thought, thrashing around in the water in search of something to hold onto.

He felt something cold and slithery beside him and squealed with horror as he tried to get away from it.

Whatever it was followed him and he heard Emma's throaty laugh. It was her tail! He quickly grabbed it, puffing with effort. Emma smiled at him and shrugged her shoulders innocently. To her it was all a game.

Lewis scrambled over to the side of the dock and looked up at Rikki and Cleo angrily.

"Great! Now I'm soaked. Fantastic idea, Rikki," he said sarcastically. "Now give me a hand out."

"I'm sorry, Lewis, but you *know* we can't do that. The mermaid thing," said Rikki, smiling

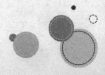

60

apologetically. "You'll have to swim around to the ladder down there," she added, pointing towards the end of the dock.

Lewis rolled his eyes and paddled in that direction.

"*You*," he ordered, pointing at Emma as he swam past her, "follow *me*."

Emma flicked her tail and swam happily behind him.

After a lot of huffing and puffing on his part, and very little help from the girls, Lewis finally managed to haul Emma out of the water and then fireman-lifted her to one of the sun-loungers on the deck, where she would be screened from view by a hedge of bushy ferns.

"We should be all right here," he said, collapsing on to the decking and gasping for air as soon as Emma was safely concealed. "At least if someone comes out looking for Emma, they won't see us from the back door; those ferns will give us good cover."

61

"Good thinking," said Cleo, smiling at him. *He thinks of everything*, she thought, pleased that someone as loyal and capable as Lewis was with them.

Emma meanwhile looked around unconcernedly.

"I can't think *why* you guys don't want to go out to Mako Island; it's so beautiful out there," she began. "But never mind, what do you want to do instead?"

Over Emma's head, ignoring her completely, Rikki, Cleo and Lewis looked at each other questioningly, each of them trying to figure out what their next move should be.

"What about if we dry you out and we go back inside and join the party, eh?" asked Rikki.

Emma shrugged. "Okay, if that's what you want, let's go." She tried to get up, but her heavy tail made it impossible and she almost tipped the sun-lounger over on its side.

"Whoah there," said Lewis, grabbing the edge of the lounger closest to him and righting

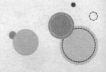

62

it again. "Not so fast, huh?"

He turned to Rikki and said, "Do your thing. You know." He held out his hand in the same way the girls did when they used their powers.

Rikki nodded and held out her own hand, palm facing Emma and thought of hot things.

The sun's rays, an oven, the fire...

It didn't take long before the water began to evaporate with the heat, causing plumes of condensation to rise from Emma's tail.

Emma leaned back and closed her eyes. "Oh that's really nice, Rikki," she giggled. "It kind of tickles."

Cleo and Lewis rolled their eyes. The sooner they got their Emma back the better! This one did nothing but give them grief!

After a couple of minutes, Rikki stopped.

"Nothing's happening. Her tail should be gone by now," she said, running her hand down Emma's tail. "She's dry but it's still there. Why isn't it *working*?"

63

"It's the full moon," said Cleo uneasily. "It's what the old lady said."

"*What* old lady?" snapped Lewis in frustration.

But before he could get an answer, Emma chimed in.

"I like my tail *just* the way it is," she smiled at the three concerned faces. "I think it's *perfect*."

Suddenly they heard the sharp *clip-clip-clip* of someone walk out onto the decking.

Aunt Thea had come out in search of Emma and had obviously heard their voices chattering behind the ferns.

"Is that you, Emma?" Thea called out.

Lewis quickly clamped his hand tightly over Emma's mouth. *The last thing we need is this one yelling out*, he thought grimly.

Cleo and Rikki jumped to their feet, their heads peeping over the ferns. There was no use pretending that there was no one out there; Aunt Thea had definitely heard voices.

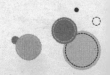

64

"No, just us," said Cleo, grinning broadly. "Cleo and Rikki getting some air."

Aunt Thea eyed the two girls suspiciously; she was sure she'd heard Emma's voice.

"I'm looking for Emma... her father's here," she said doubtfully, wondering why the two girls were outside when they were meant to be inside handing around drinks and nibbles.

Cleo glanced down at Lewis, who with a nod of his head indicated that she and Rikki should go over to Aunt Thea before she came down to investigate what they were up to!

Cleo nudged Rikki and the two girls walked around the ferns and up to Aunt Thea, standing either side of her and trying hard to act as innocently as possible.

"Beautiful night," Cleo began conversationally.

Rikki nodded, smiling at Aunt Thea.

"Just watch out for bats," she added, thinking quickly.

"*Bats?*" asked Aunt Thea, looking nervously

up into the black night as if she suddenly expected to see a bat swooping towards her.

From his position hunkered down beside Emma, Lewis started to worry.

If the moon comes out and the girls go la-la again, we're in big trouble, he thought uneasily. *Maybe if I can sneak around to the back door, using these ferns as cover, I'll be able to get Emma's aunt to go inside. I could say that Emma's father is looking for her or something. But of course that means I'll have to leave Emma here on her own... and I don't know if she can be trusted in her present state.*

He glanced at Emma, who still lay relaxing in the sun-lounger, tapping her tail rhythmically and looking completely indifferent to what was happening around her.

I'm going to have to risk it, he thought, peering up into the sky and seeing that the clouds were thinning out to the east and that it was only a matter of time before the moon revealed itself.

Slowly he peeled his hand off Emma's

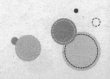

66

mouth and glared at her, willing her to keep quiet. But again, she seemed not to notice and feeling a little more confident that she'd keep her mouth shut, Lewis snuck off down the deck, careful to keep his back lower than the line of plants. He knew he'd be able to double back to the door when he got to the spa-pool; it was only a matter of whether the moon would stay hidden until he got there!

Meanwhile, Cleo and Rikki were still trying to scare Aunt Thea inside with stories of bats.

"There's a lot out tonight. *Swarms* of bats," said Rikki, staring up into the empty sky and wishing a flock of them would dive bomb the deck now to illustrate her point. "There's *thousands* of them actually," she added, nodding her head wisely as if she knew the flight path of every bat in the greater Gold Coast area.

And it was working! Aunt Thea looked from Rikki to Cleo and back again. She didn't like bats and ordinarily she would have immediately

67

turned on her heels and marched inside, but there was something mysterious going on and Aunt Thea wanted to get to the bottom of it!

Suddenly they heard a rustling sound, which caused Aunt Thea to jump in fright.

Is that a bat?! she asked herself, unconsciously backing away toward the door.

But instead they saw the ferns below them waving slightly before parting to reveal Emma's mischievous face looking up at them.

Cleo and Rikki both inhaled sharply, their eyes wide with terror as they fought the temptation to look at Aunt Thea and see what *she* was doing. They both knew they couldn't reveal that they'd lied to her – it was much better to just stick with the 'gosh we had no idea she was there' plan they'd already half-concocted.

"Hi Aunt Thea," Emma called cheerily. "Do you want to come to Mako Island with me?"

Beside them, Rikki and Cleo felt Aunt Thea stiffen and glare accusingly at each of them in turn.

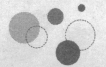
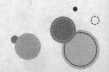

Okay, we've been caught lying to an old biddy. I don't care about that, but where's Lewis?! thought Rikki angrily, *he's meant to be keeping an eye on Emma.*

But it was too late to start blaming anybody; Aunt Thea had seen Emma and that was that!

Thankfully from where they stood on the decking, most of Emma's body was still hidden behind the ferns; it was only her face that they could see properly. But it wouldn't take much for Aunt Thea to walk down the three remaining steps and around the ferns... *oh that doesn't bear thinking about!* thought Cleo anxiously, fighting every impulse to simply run inside and away from the situation. *Emma is my best friend; I have to stay. It doesn't matter what happens, we've got to stick together.*

The ferns parted abruptly in a different spot further away from Emma and Lewis's face peeked out at them.

"Hey! Hi!" he called loudly, trying to draw Aunt Thea's attention away from Emma, "Emma's not exactly herself tonight."

69

He shrugged and smiled broadly before one of the ferns snapped back and hit him in the face. After a bit more thrashing about out behind the ferns, Lewis's face popped up again next Emma's and he pulled her back out of view.

That was the last straw for Aunt Thea.

First these two girls tell me a whole lot of fibs and then I find my niece in the back yard with a young man acting strangely and talking gibberish!

"What are Neil and Lisa *doing* with that child?" she said in a horrified tone, before whirling around on her heels and stomping indoors in disgust. *It's not the time to say it now, but I think a family conference is called for!*

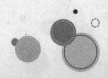

70

Chapter 6

No one moved until they heard the back door slam shut behind the angry Aunt Thea.

"*Phew*, that was close," Cleo said, letting out a long sigh of relief as she and Rikki ran back around to join the others.

The three friends squatted down beside Emma again, who smiled merrily and flapped her tail a bit harder. *We're having so much fun tonight!* she giggled to herself.

"We need to do something before everyone else starts looking for her," said Rikki, trying to formulate a plan.

Cleo pulled the party itinerary out of her pocket, read down the list, checking her watch at the same time to see what was due to happen next.

"Okay it's nine-eight. According to the schedule, Elliot plays oboe until nine-ten pm.

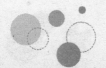

71

That means we have two minutes," she said, looking to Lewis and Rikki for ideas.

Without warning they suddenly heard a weird, other-worldly gurgling sound. It was coming from the direction of Emma's stomach!

"I need to eat something *now*," she complained, rubbing her tummy. "I'm *soooo* starving. I need food!"

"Sardines!" said Cleo, suddenly remembering she still had them in her pocket where she'd stashed them before running out of the kitchen earlier.

She quickly handed them to Emma, who without delay, ripped off the lid and gobbled them down one by one, moaning with delight.

Lewis, Cleo and Rikki watched her silently, wrinkling their noses as the overpowering smell wafted over them. Even Cleo, whose dad worked on the fishing boats, found it disgusting!

That is so gross! thought Rikki, her stomach churning as each sardine was hastily despatched.

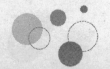

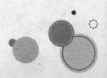

"Er… *anyway*," Lewis began, finding it difficult to tear his eyes away from the sight of Emma gulping down the sardines, "we need to put Emma somewhere safe and get back to the party. They're going to be suspicious if we *all* disappear. That's if Aunt Thea hasn't mentioned seeing Emma out here already."

"Oh great, Einstein, don't you think they're going to be suspicious anyway when Emma's a no-show at her dad's birthday?" snapped Rikki.

"Well, have you got any *better* ideas?" Lewis asked angrily.

"Guys. *Guys*. We haven't got time for this," said Cleo reasonably, trying to stop the argument before it had properly begun. "Let's get Emma out of this sun-lounger before Aunt Thea comes out with a search party."

Lewis and Rikki looked at each other narrowly, their jaws tightening.

"Hmph!" said Rikki.

"*Fine!*" Lewis snapped. "Let's put her in the spa-pool. At least that way she's likely to be

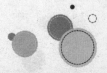

73

quiet." He looked meaningfully at Emma as he said the last two words.

Emma, completely unaware of the trouble she was causing her friends, simply poked out her tongue and laughed uproariously.

With Cleo at Emma's head, Rikki holding her middle and Lewis picking up her heavy tail, they managed to heave her over to the spa and into the water.

"I'll go and put the lights and the jets on," said Lewis; "I don't think you'll be able to see Emma's tail so easily with the water bubbling around and with any luck the glare of the bright lights will blind anyone looking straight down into the pool."

"Good idea," Rikki nodded, their argument already forgotten.

Lewis ran off to the wash-house, leaving Cleo and Rikki standing by the spa looking down at Emma.

"Don't make *any* noise, just stay here," said Rikki as if talking to a child.

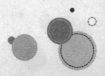

74

Suddenly the spa started up and Emma wiggled happily in the water and threw Rikki and Cleo a coy glance as if to say *Me? Make a lot of noise?*

They rolled their eyes and made to go inside before they were stopped by Lewis hurrying back towards them.

"Guys, I can't go in there looking like *this*," he yelped, holding his arms out to indicate his soaked clothes.

"That's alright," Rikki grinned. "How do you feel about being... *steam-dried*?"

Lewis sighed resignedly. He didn't like the idea of Rikki unleashing her powers upon him; it seemed to him that she didn't *really* have a handle on how to use them properly just yet. But what alternative did he have?

"Okay," he sighed again. "Where do you want me?"

Rikki and Cleo looked at each other.

"Emma's room. It'll be the safest place because anyone that's looking for Emma has

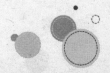

75

already looked in there for her," said Cleo, using more logic in those few words than Rikki had ever heard her use in the whole time they'd been friends.

Impressive, Rikki thought to herself, *maybe this whole moon-spell thing is working on Cleo in reverse. Ordinarily she's kind of scatter-brained and ditzy, but that idea was like something Emma would usually come up with.* She glanced back at the spa-pool, where Emma was humming softly to herself and waving her arms back and forth beneath the water. *With the emphasis on 'usually'*, Rikki added gloomily.

"Plus, I can see from here that one of the side windows is open a crack so we can get in that way without having to walk through the party," added Cleo, pleased with her newly-discovered planning skills.

"Well let's get on with it then," said Lewis, going over to the window and lifting up the sash. He climbed in, closely followed by Cleo and Rikki.

76

A second after Rikki had closed the window behind her, Byron came around the corner.

Emma had told him that the quickest way from his place to the party would be via the tow-path that ran alongside the canal, but now that he was there, he couldn't find a way into the party. He had been scrambling around in the bushes at the back of the house for the last ten minutes!

There must be a door around here somewhere, he thought to himself. Suddenly he heard his name being called.

"*By-ron*," Emma cooed seductively as she caught sight of him strolling along the path. "I'm over *here*, Byron."

He spun around and spied her in the spa, her arms resting on ground with her chin resting on her hands, smiling brightly up at him.

"Cool, you've got the spa going," grinned Bryon, leaning casually against the veranda and taking care to show her his best side. "How's the water?"

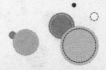

77

"Come over here and I'll show you," Emma replied, beckoning him over.

Byron raised his eyebrows slightly and gave Emma a playful look. He'd never seen this side of Emma and he liked what he saw... *a lot!*

"Come *closer*, Byron..." said Emma, pushing off from the side of the spa and tilting her head down slightly before looking back up at him through her eyelashes.

Byron moved slowly over to the spa pool and knelt down beside it.

"Come *closer*..." Emma repeated flirtatiously, leaning towards him until their faces almost met.

Byron gave Emma his sexiest smile and tilted his face closer to hers until their lips were just about touching when suddenly he pulled back and screwed up his nose.

"Have you being eating *sardines*?" he asked, sniffing her breath.

But Emma just smiled and closed her eyes, half-lifting her upper body out of the

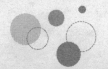
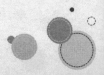

water until she found his lips and kissed them passionately.

Behind them Elliot appeared, still holding his oboe. He'd been sent out by his mother to find Emma and he'd found her all right! Elliot stared in astonishment before hastily doing an about-face and rushing back inside to find Cleo and Rikki. He could hardly tell his *mother* that Emma was in the spa-pool kissing his surfing instructor!

He found both girls in the kitchen, pouring more drinks for the guests.

"I've found Emma," he puffed, out of breath from running. "She's outside in the spa."

"You *talked* to her?" asked Rikki trying to keep the worry out of her voice.

"No... she was sort of... *busy*," replied Elliot hesitantly, screwing up his nose with embarrassment. "... *kissing Byron*."

Cleo's heart leaped into her throat and she felt sick.

79

Uh-oh, things have suddenly got a lot more dangerous… she thought to herself, before gently pushing Elliot to one side and dashing outside. *I hope we're not too late!*

Rikki patted Elliot on the head in a sisterly kind of way and raced out after Cleo. She hoped Elliot hadn't been too traumatized by what he'd seen happening in the spa!

Elliot just stood there and watched the girls leave; he was happy for the situation to be in someone else's hands now. *Yuck!* he shuddered. *Kissing!*

Rikki was hardly out the door before she heard Cleo hollering out towards the spa, "Stop right there!"

Her tone clearly caused Byron to panic and he leaped to his feet in mid-kiss.

"I'm cool," he squeaked nervously, before seeing that it was only Cleo and not Emma's mother, as he'd feared. He relaxed again. "Interesting party," he drawled, eyeing Emma suggestively.

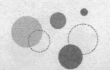
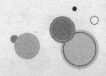

Rikki came over to the side of the spa-pool and looked at Emma in amazement. She couldn't believe this was the same clean-living Emma that she'd been friends with all these months.

"See you later, Byron," said Emma flirtatiously, giving him a little wave.

"I like where this party is going," grinned Byron, giving her a wink before turning to go inside.

Cleo and Rikki watched him leave and gazed down at Emma, wondering what they could possibly do to keep her out of more mischief.

"We need to get her to her bedroom and lock her in," said Rikki.

"We can't exactly take her past everyone on a sun-lounger," Cleo said exasperatedly.

At that moment there was a cough from behind them. Both girls spun around, but it was only Lewis.

He was wheeling Emma's grandma's

wheelchair in front of him and wearing a big grin.

"We could use *this*…" he offered.

The girls grinned back.

"Brilliant idea!" said Cleo enthusiastically. "Let's get her into it before we run into *more* trouble."

After more huffing and puffing, they managed to pull Emma out of the spa-pool and into the wheelchair. By putting Rikki's jacket over her and tucking Grandma's rug around her tail, they all agreed that she looked like she might have legs under there somewhere.

Emma seemed quite happy to get out of the spa too, particularly after they told her that she could go in and join the party.

"Okay, now we can't stop for anyone," said Lewis matter-of-factly. "If anyone asks, we're taking Emma upstairs because she's not feeling well. The plan is to take her through the kitchen and straight to the bathroom and then leave her in there."

82

In fact he'd already checked out all the possibilities before he'd even taken the wheelchair. After Rikki had dried him off, he'd circulated amongst the guests and noticed that everyone was using the downstairs bathroom closest to the kitchen. That left the upstairs bathroom free. All they had to do was carry the wheelchair up a short flight of stairs and they'd be safe.

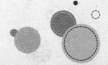

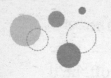
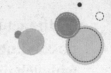

Chapter 7

Aunt Thea sat at the kitchen table and drummed her fingers. She wondered if she should say something to Lisa and Neil about Emma's odd behaviour. Suddenly her thoughts were interrupted by the sight of Emma being pushed through the kitchen in a wheelchair by her strange friends.

Her jaw dropped and she shook her head disappointedly. *Joy-riding around the party in her own grandmother's wheelchair...* she mentally tut-tutted.

"Rather tasteless humour," she called after them snootily, as Emma gave her a friendly wave in passing.

"Okay, we're over the first hurdle," Lewis whispered grimly as he kept an eye on Aunt Thea to make sure she wasn't following them.

Cleo, right behind him, glanced back. It was all right; Aunt Thea hadn't made a move to get

84

up. "Keep going, Lewis, we're going to make it," she said encouragingly, as they reached the hallway.

Then they spied Byron. He stood in the hall doorway, his back to them as he surveyed the party crowd.

"Uh, second hurdle alert, second hurdle alert," Lewis murmured softly.

Cleo and Rikki, following close behind him, had spotted Byron too.

If we can just make it past him... Rikki thought, glancing at Emma to check whether she'd seen him, *then it's just up the stairs and we're all good.*

But Emma *had* seen Byron and as Lewis wheeled her past, she reached out and pinched his bottom!

Lewis gulped and accelerated down the hall and around the corner out of sight. Byron swung around in time to see Cleo pass behind him.

85

"*Cleo*," said Byron, a big grinning spreading across his beautiful face; he was surprised to see that it was her who had grabbed him! "Good to see you too."

Cleo smiled innocently back at him. She didn't know what he was talking about, but just as long as he wasn't interested in what they were up to, she didn't care!

Byron, totally misunderstanding her smile, beamed back.

I don't know what they've put in the punch, but this party is turning out to be more fun than I'd thought it'd be! he said to himself.

Around the corner in the hallway, Emma suddenly yanked the brake on the wheelchair, causing her friends to collide into each other like toppling dominoes.

She grinned broadly, for right in front of them stood Zane and Miriam... *kissing!*

They all watched silently, their mouths agape at the horror of it all, until Rikki eventually broke the spell by miming sticking

86

her finger down her throat and making gagging noises.

Cleo giggled. *Even in a dangerous situation like this, Rikki still manages to keep her sense of humour*, she thought admiringly.

But still Miriam and Zane continued kissing, oblivious to the fact they were being watched.

In fact, they were so busy, they wouldn't have noticed if their own parents had walked into the hallway, which they very well could've considering they were *at* the party!

Without warning, Emma quickly stuck out her hand and using her powers, froze their lips together in an icy-cold kiss.

Ice to meet you, she said to herself, laughing aloud, before Lewis hastily threw the brake off and wheeled her towards the flight of stairs.

Miriam and Zane felt the biting cold immediately and not understanding what was happening, struggled to break free of each other, but the ice had stuck their lips fast!

87

Panicked, Miriam put her hands on Zane's shoulders and tried to push him away. "Mmmmmmph," Zane yowled in pain.

"Mmmph mmmmmmmph," replied Miriam, her eyes widening in surprise.

In the lounge, Mrs Gilbert heard Emma's laugh and poked her head out into the hallway in time to see Lewis parking the wheelchair at the bottom of the steps.

"Em? *Emma*?" she said. "It's time to make your speech, darling."

Emma shuffled around and waved at her mother over the back of the wheelchair as Cleo and Rikki jumped between them in an effort to shield their friend from her mother's searching look.

"Emma's asked me to do it," Cleo blurted out, thinking on her feet. "She's a bit… nervous."

"*Really*? That's not like her," said Mrs Gilbert, suddenly aware that the guests were hovering around the doorway sensing that

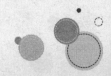

88

something interesting was about to happen.

Cleo looked over her shoulder as Rikki and Lewis disappeared up the stairs with the wheelchair.

"Actually she *begged* me to do it," said Cleo, trying to sound both confident and convincing and, she suspected, failing dismally!

Mrs Gilbert looked searchingly at Cleo. She wasn't sure what was going on, but she definitely smelled a rat.

But after Emma's past behaviour this evening, perhaps she has *asked Cleo to read her speech...* she thought to herself.

"Well... I *suppose*..." she began, looking at her husband, who merely shrugged.

He hadn't been there to see Emma's earlier performance, so he was completely in the dark about what was happening.

And that short delay was all Cleo needed.

"Excuse me everybody," she began, her voice raised to make sure she had all the guests'

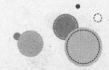

89

attention. "I'd like to make a speech… on behalf of Emma… to her father."

She smiled sweetly at Mr Gilbert.

Upstairs, Lewis held the door open as Rikki pushed Emma into the bathroom. They were tired after the effort of carrying the heavy wheelchair, and the even heavier Emma, up the flight of stairs, but they knew they had to hurry and get back downstairs to rescue Cleo.

"What's she going to *say*?" whispered Lewis, over Emma's head.

"Well… she did hear a *bit* of Emma's speech this morning – she should be okay," Rikki replied doubtfully, looking around the bathroom. She gave Emma one last smile before closing the door behind her.

As they stood outside the bathroom door, Rikki and Lewis heard Cleo's words drift up the stairs.

"Dear Mr Gilbert… *Dad.* Happy birthday to the most magnificent, deadly…no," they

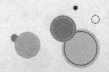

90

heard Cleo falter and imagined her furiously wracking her brains to remember the speech. "… *debonair*…"

"Hurry," said Rikki, grabbing Lewis by the sleeve and dragging him behind her. "We need to get down there *now*."

Emma frowned at the closed door.

How dare they just leave me here! I thought I was going to a party, but instead I'm locked in a bathroom with nothing but a bathtub full of… oh, hold on a minute.

Emma wheeled herself over to the bath and sniffed at the foil-covered platters.

In seconds she'd ripped one open. In front of her was a smorgasbord of the best seafood Cleo's father could supply!

Emma laughed delightedly. *Perhaps it's not so bad after all…*

Downstairs, Mr and Mrs Gilbert exchanged confused glances as Cleo stumbled on with Emma's speech.

"… something, *something*…" mumbled

91

Cleo, eyes skyward as she desperately tried to remember something, *anything* from Emma's practice run-through earlier that day. "Um... ah..." Cleo stumbled, before finally recalling something useful. "... *kindest* dad in the whole world."

She clapped her hands, pleased that she was back on track.

"Where would the world be without dads? There'd be a lot more room for everybody," Cleo continued animatedly, laughing at her own joke.

The guests looked at each other and then Mr Gilbert as silence descended over the room.

"Just joking," said Cleo doubtfully.

I'm losing the crowd! thought Cleo, feeling the panic rising in her chest. She took a couple of deep breaths. *I'm doing this for Emma, I have to remember that.*

"Dads... where would the world *be* without dads?" she tried again.

Suddenly Cleo had the guests' full attention!

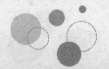

92

Everyone was focusing intently on her again.

Or so *she* thought. What she didn't know was that Zane and Miriam, in their struggle to break their icy lip-lock, had accidentally stumbled out of the hall and were now tussling about right behind her! The guests weren't watching Cleo, they were following the extraordinary events unfolding behind her back!

Ominously, they began to murmur...

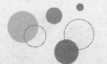

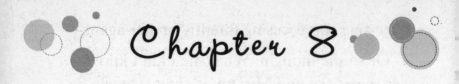

Chapter 8

Mrs Gilbert had had enough! Turning to Elliot, who stood dumbstruck between his parents, she whispered, "Elliot, please go upstairs and bring down the seafood platters. *Now.*"

Elliot ran through the kitchen, narrowly avoiding being knocked over by Zane as he tried unsuccessfully to fight off Miriam. He was halfway up the stairs when he ran into Rikki and Lewis coming down the other way.

"Have either of you seen Emma?" Elliot asked.

"She needs quiet, she's in the bathroom," Rikki replied, before adding, "doing some yoga."

That is possibly the lamest excuse I've ever come up with! Rikki thought in silent fury. *Great! Emma goes boy-crazy, Cleo gets logical and I get... lame?? Fan-tas-tic!*

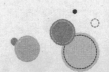

94

Elliot looked at them, puzzled by Rikki's and Lewis's behaviour. In the sudden silence that descended, Rikki, Lewis and Elliot could hear Cleo's voice float up to them from downstairs.

"Mr Gilbert is thoughtful too," she was saying. "I remember once, when I was twelve, he made me a cheese sandwich. Even though I'm lactose intolerant and vomited it up. It's the thought that counts."

Mr Gilbert felt his face flush with embarrassment. *This is meant to be a surprise party and it certainly is full of surprises!!* he thought to himself as he plastered on another fake smile in an effort to show he wasn't offended by Cleo's little story.

"Plus he's quite a good dresser... for an *older* person," Cleo continued, beginning to feel desperate. She had no idea how she was going to get out of the hole she'd dug for herself.

Lewis and Rikki exchanged glances. They needed to get out there to save Cleo, but if

95

they went downstairs now, they knew there was every chance Elliot would go into the bathroom and see Emma. Of course, it was possible that Elliot would just waltz into the bathroom, take the seafood and leave again without even talking to Emma, but knowing how close Emma and Elliot were, Rikki and Lewis both knew what a slim possibility that was.

"But how am I meant to get the seafood platters out?" enquired Elliot, wishing they'd just get out of the way and let him do his job.

"They're in the *bathroom*?" said Rikki. *I hope I hope I hope Emma hasn't found them...*

Elliot nodded. "I've been sent up to get them," he said.

"*Okaay*... just give us a minute on that one," Rikki said, grabbing Lewis's arm and dashing back to the bathroom.

Rikki threw the door open and Lewis ran in to see Emma sitting innocently where they'd left her.

"Everything okay?" he asked.

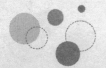

96

"Yes – *hic* – thank you," Emma smiled as she attempted to smother a hiccup.

"Good," Lewis smiled back, rushing over to the bath and hastily scooping up the three silver-foiled platters.

It doesn't look like Emma had enough time to get her hands on the food at least! Lewis thought with relief, as he carried them out to Elliot.

"All yours," he said, handing them over.

Elliot took the platters, nodded his thanks and went back downstairs.

Rikki and Lewis looked at each other and smiled. They'd got away with it!

Downstairs, Cleo could see that the guests were becoming increasingly restless the longer she went on speaking. It seemed like now would be as good a time as any to wrap the speech up.

"So, in closing, I'd like to say, thanks Mr Gilbert... for being a dad."

Cleo paused for a moment and when no one

97

made a move, quickly added. "You can clap now, I've finished."

She smiled broadly as one by one the guests began to clap hesitantly. It was like *they* were spellbound!

Cleo gave a little curtsey, spun on her heels and taking the stairs two at a time rushed up to the bathroom.

Emma's parents watched her go.

I'm sure Cleo meant well, thought Mrs Gilbert charitably, *but that was the oddest birthday speech I've ever heard!*

She spied Elliot taking the platters into the kitchen and heaved a sigh of relief. Turning to her guests she announced proudly, "Ladies and gentleman, if you'd like to make your way through to the kitchen, dinner will be served shortly."

With the Gilberts at the lead, the visitors slowly made their way through to the kitchen, all of them eager to sample some of the culinary delights they were sure would be on offer.

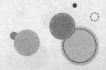

98

Cleo gently knocked on the bathroom door and before she could get a reply, opened the door and shut it quickly behind her.

Rikki, Lewis and Emma looked over at her expectantly.

"How did the speech go?" Lewis asked, breaking the silence.

"Pretty well I think," said Cleo, beginning to relax. "I couldn't remember Emma's speech word for word of course, but I improvised and Mr Gilbert seemed to like it!"

Rikki and Lewis grinned at each other. They both felt that they'd had the easier job in looking after Emma – neither of them would have had a clue what to say in front of a room full of people!

"Good for you," said Rikki proudly. "You'll have to fill us in on the details later though, because right now we've got other fish to fry." She gestured to Emma, who started and looked at her with annoyance.

"Oh sorry Em, bad choice of words!" Rikki apologized hastily.

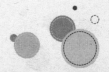

99

"I think perhaps it'd be better if we put you somewhere more comfortable," said Cleo, changing the subject quickly and giving Emma a friendly smile.

"Can I go down to the party?" Emma asked, looking from Cleo to Rikki hopefully.

"Well... maybe later," Cleo replied. "But for now, how about if we just hang out in your room?" Lewis opened the door a crack to see if anyone was hanging around in the hallway.

"All clear," he said finally, opening the door wider and ushering the girls out of the bathroom.

"I don't want to go in here," complained Emma as they wheeled her across the hallway and into her bedroom. "I want to go swimming, it's so much nicer in the water!"

"Stay here while we cover for you and don't make a sound, okay?" he said, patting Emma reassuringly on the shoulder and making for the door.

Cleo stared down at Emma with regret. *If only it had been me who was moonstruck!* she

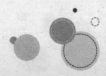

100

thought unhappily. *Then Emma could have at least gone to the party, instead of being hidden away in her bedroom!*

"We'll be back soon, Em, promise," she added softly.

The two girls followed Lewis out and shut the door.

"I hope she stays put," said Rikki grimly.

Emma heard the door click shut and stared at it, wishing someone would come in and keep her company.

I don't see why I shouldn't go to the party, it's boring in here, she thought, glancing around the room and searching for something to do.

She wheeled herself over to the door and tried the doorknob. She could turn it, so she knew they hadn't locked her in, but she couldn't actually *open* the door wide enough to get out because the wheelchair was in the way.

Frustrated, Emma wheeled herself back to the centre of the room.

I'll just have to crawl down to the party, she

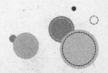

101

thought determinedly as she leaned forward as far as she could until – *PLOP!* – Emma found herself on the floor.

This is a good start! she thought gleefully, as she used her strong swimmer's arms to pull herself across the carpet. *Now I'm getting somewhere!*

Emma reached the door and stretching up as far as she could, she turned the doorknob and opened the door a crack, just in time to hear footsteps passing by her bedroom!

It was Byron, grinning to himself and humming a little tune. *This is some party*, he thought, laughing as he recalled Cleo's speech.

He had just reached the bathroom door when he heard someone softly calling his name.

"Byron..."

He turned and looked down the hallway, but there was no one there!

"Byron," Emma called again as she opened the door a little wider and pulled herself further into the hallway.

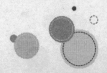

He looked down this time to see Emma smiling up at him.

"Sorry about the interruption before," she giggled.

"So am I," Byron smiled.

"There's no one here to interrupt us now, why don't you come closer." Emma said invitingly.

Byron raised his eyebrows in surprise. He had no idea Emma was so much fun! She'd always struck him as really nice girl, and beautiful of course, but tonight... well tonight she seemed *different* somehow...

He got down on his knees and lay down in the hallway, his long legs crammed up against the bathroom door, until their faces were only inches apart and he was looking directly into Emma's big blue eyes.

Their lips met in a long lingering kiss and although Byron couldn't see it, Emma's tail flapped happily on the carpet behind her.

They lay like that for some moments before

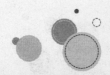

103

they suddenly heard a footfall on the stairs.

This time it was Aunt Thea and what a surprise *she* got when she came around the stairwell corner into the hall!

She gave a little cough that caused Emma and Byron to stop abruptly and glance up to see who had interrupted them.

"*Another* boy," said Aunt Thea between pursed lips as she glared down at her niece in disgust.

But Emma just beamed back at her, giving a little wave and shrugging her shoulders as if she didn't mind a bit that her Aunt had caught her.

Byron, his head resting on his hands, smiled too.

From behind Aunt Thea, Rikki, Cleo and Lewis suddenly hovered into view. Rikki had seen Aunt Thea heading up the stairs and had signalled to the other two what was about to happen.

Suddenly the narrow hallway was packed with people!

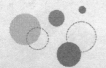

104

"Byron, dinner's ready," Cleo blurted out, trying to think of a way to get Aunt Thea and Byron back downstairs. "Better hurry up before it's all gone."

Byron looked at Emma apologetically and kissed her quickly on the nose before getting slowly to his feet.

"Later," he said, smiling happily as he squeezed past everyone on his way to the head of the stairs.

"Wait for me, I'm coming," Emma called, floundering around on the floor in an effort to get out of her bedroom and into the hall.

Aunt Thea glared at her, looked skywards, and after muttering something under her breath, followed Byron back down to the party.

"We can't hold her like this for much longer," said Lewis as he watched Emma rolling about on the floor.

Rikki nodded her head in agreement. *That was too close; if Byron had just peeked through the crack in the door...*

105

"So the bedroom wasn't the *best* idea," she said aloud, wracking her brain for what to do next.

They were running out of places to hide Emma!

Cleo meanwhile had opened the door and was gently helping Emma up from the floor.

Lewis suddenly jumped to his feet. "I've got a key for The Juice-Net Café," he whispered excitedly.

"How did you get that?" asked Cleo as she and Rikki struggled to get Emma back into the wheelchair.

"Wilfred hired me to fix his internet connections," said Lewis.

They looked at each other and down at Emma. No one would search for her at the Juice-Net – it was perfect!

Emma grinned happily; it looked like she was going to get to go somewhere fun after all.

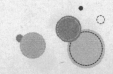

Chapter 9

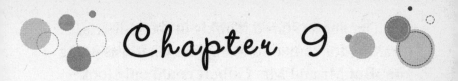

Back in the kitchen, the guests all stood in a semi-circle around the bench top, clutching their plates and hungrily eyeing the platters as Mrs Gilbert peeled back the silver foil.

It had been a long, strange night and they were ready to eat!

Slowly Mrs Gilbert unwrapped the first plate... but aside from a few stray fish bones and lemon quarters, it was completely empty!

She frowned and attacked the foil on the next dish, tearing it open hurriedly. Empty crab shells and a half eaten lobster!

And the third dish was the same – everything was eaten up!

What's going on? she thought angrily. *Is this someone's idea of a joke?!*

She turned to her husband, her eyes wide with surprise as she felt her face turn red with embarrassment.

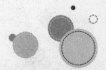

The guests stared blankly at the Gilberts, waiting for someone to explain what was going on. But Mr and Mrs Gilbert could only look back at them blankly. They didn't know what to say because they didn't know what was going on themselves!

It was Dr Bennett who finally broke the uncomfortable silence.

"Personally I'm not that hungry anyway. I had a big lunch… *eight hours ago*," he spat sarcastically. He turned to Candy and gestured angrily to her that they were leaving.

Murmuring quietly amongst themselves, the party guests filed out to collect their coats and go home. Soon there were only the Gilberts and Aunt Thea left in the kitchen.

"I believe that daughter of yours needs a good dose of old fashioned discipline," snapped Aunt Thea nastily, before bustling off to collect her mother.

Mrs Gilbert's eyes flashed in anger. She was just about to snap back at her sister-in-law when she realized it wouldn't make any difference what she said. Tiredly she leaned

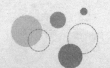

against the kitchen bench and watched Aunt Thea leave. *Emma?* she thought to herself, slightly perplexed. *They're blaming Emma for what happened tonight?*

It had never occurred to her that Emma would sabotage her own much-loved father's birthday party... *after all the work she put in... it's impossible, I know it is!*

But what *had* happened, that's what she wanted to know. That's what they *all* wanted to know!

Emma's parents stood quietly in the kitchen until they heard the door slam shut behind the last of the visitors. Then they raced upstairs to Emma's bedroom.

"This girl has some explaining to do," said Mr Gilbert angrily as he flung open Emma's bedroom door without knocking.

The curtain on the open window fluttered in the warm night breeze; the room was empty!

109

Chapter 10

Lewis leaned against the counter at The Juice-Net Café and gulped down air, trying desperately to get his breath back. Not only had his arms been strained to the limit when they'd lowered Emma down to the garden from her bedroom window wrapped in bed-sheets, but then he'd walked all the way from the party with the still-wrapped-up Emma slung over his shoulders. His legs were still wobbly from it all.

Thankfully, Emma had tired herself out with all the scrambling around she'd done on her bedroom floor and had fallen asleep as soon as they'd left the house. Getting her to the café hadn't been as hard as Lewis had feared.

As soon as they'd let themselves in, they'd quietly laid her down on the pool table, as it was the only surface long enough to hold her comfortably. She hadn't stirred since.

"We should really all try and get some sleep ourselves," Lewis had whispered to Rikki and

Cleo, "it's been a long evening."

The girls yawned and nodded in silent agreement, searching around for some chairs to push together to use as makeshift beds as Lewis stumbled across the café floor and collapsed into the nearest booth.

"Goodnight, guys," he mumbled as he snuggled down into the vinyl upholstery and promptly fell asleep.

Rikki stood by the door waiting until Cleo was ready and then flicked off the light switch. Gingerly she felt her way through the dark to her own improvised bed.

"Night, Cleo," she said quietly.

"Night, Rikki," Cleo replied softly.

The moon was sinking lower on the horizon, but even in the dim light it was now casting, Rikki could see that Cleo's eyes were open and she was watching Emma.

"She'll be okay, Cleo," said Rikki in a low voice, trying to reassure her.

"I hope so, Rikki, I really do," replied Cleo. Slowly, her eyes closed.

The night passed slowly for the two girls. Neither of them could get comfortable on their chairs and even listening to Emma's low regular breathing couldn't relax them enough to fall asleep. Occasionally they'd hear little yaps from Lewis's direction too, which didn't help matters.

I wonder what Lewis is dreaming about, thought Cleo idly at one point, before drifting off into her own half-awake/half-asleep dream state.

Some time later, Cleo noticed the room was starting to get lighter. The sun hadn't come up yet, but she could just make out different shapes in the room. She could see the outline of Lewis in the booth, breathing rhythmically, and felt a stab of envy as she thought how easily he slept.

Beside her Cleo heard Rikki give a little grunt and turn restlessly on her chair.

"Have you been asleep?" she whispered.

"No," Rikki replied tiredly, her face squashed against the seat of the chair, lines from the vinyl criss-crossing her cheek.

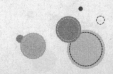

"Me neither," said Cleo glumly, stretching out her aching limbs.

She looked over at Emma who was lying fast asleep in the same position they'd left her the previous night. Her long tail hung over the end of the pool table, grazing the floor. She was still a mermaid.

"What if she's stuck like this forever? What if her tail never goes away?" Cleo asked suddenly, her voice full of dread. All through the night she'd tried to keep positive, believing that when they woke up, their Emma would be back, legs and all. But now it was almost dawn and Emma hadn't changed one bit.

"There's always the circus," mumbled Lewis, still half asleep.

Rikki and Cleo threw him dirty looks, but it was too dark to see anything. Lewis, hearing no reply, turned over in the booth and went back to sleep.

Cleo rested her head on her arm and closed her eyes. She couldn't remember ever having been quite so tired...

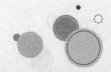

113

An hour later, while everyone was finally sleeping soundly in the Juice-Net, the moon shone the last of its silvery beams out over the water and finally dipped below the horizon. In the east, the sun took its cue and rose brightly, causing the birds to begin their morning chirrups and the possums and other night animals to retreat to their burrows to sleep out the day.

The trill of a particularly insistent king parrot infiltrated Emma's dream and she woke up slowly, stretching out her arms and yawning.

"I had the *best* sleep," she said as she sat upright on the pool table and arched her back until it gave a little click.

Rikki and Cleo, propped up on their elbows, looked over at her. They smiled as Emma slowly stretched her long legs out in front of her and rotated her ankles, trying to get some feeling back into her feet.

Suddenly Emma's eyes snapped open and her jaw dropped as she finally where she was.

"What am I doing here, guys?" she asked, all traces of tiredness gone.

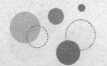
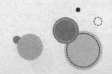

114

Cleo, Rikki and Lewis exchanged exhausted looks but said nothing. No one knew where to start!

Emma looked at them expectantly. She could remember going into the kitchen to bring out the punch, but after that everything was a blur. She was dying to know how they'd ended up at the Juice-Net Café!

But her friends' expressions said it all; even without hearing a single word of explanation about last night's events, somehow Emma knew she'd behaved weirdly. Inside she felt the cringe of embarrassment.

"What *happened*?" she asked hesitantly, although she didn't really want to know the gory details.

"It's a *long* story," Rikki winced.

"Oh no, is it... humiliating?" Emma asked tentatively.

"Yes," said Lewis decidedly. "*Very.*"

115

Chapter 11

Emma padded up the steps in her bare feet and walked into the entrance hall of her home. From the kitchen she heard the sound of someone moving about and the rustle of plastic bags. She hesitated outside the kitchen for a moment before gathering up the courage to go through.

I can't put it off, I have to face my parents; they must've been worried sick about me! she thought guiltily.

Emma stood in the doorway and watched her father scraping the remains of what looked and smelled like seafood spring-rolls into the bin before walking a circuit around the kitchen and collecting up empty glasses. *Spring-rolls*, thought Emma, allowing herself some idle thoughts before facing the music, *why do I feel like I never want to eat spring-rolls again? Or sardines for that matter?* Her thoughts were

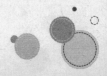

interrupted by the sound of glass clinking against crystal as she watched her dad reaching behind the toaster to grab another champagne flute. He still hadn't noticed Emma standing there.

"Dad, don't worry about that. I've organized for a cleaning company to come around," she said simply.

Mr Gilbert looked up quickly as soon as he heard his daughter's voice.

"Where have you been? I've been up half the night looking for you," he said, his voice an equal mix of anger and relief.

Emma hung her head sorrowfully. She knew he was disappointed in her and that was the worst feeling of all.

"I'm really sorry, I... I can't even explain it," stuttered Emma sadly, wishing she could tell him the truth so that he knew how the whole thing had been beyond her control.

Mr Gilbert put down the plate he'd been holding and came around to the other side

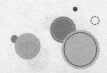

of the kitchen counter. He wanted to hug Emma and tell her she could tell him what had happened – he wouldn't judge her – but something stopped him from saying it.

"So many strange things happened," Emma began falteringly, going into the lounge and sitting down on the couch. "And I'm sorry I acted so weird. Maybe it's a teenage thing."

Mr Gilbert came over and sat down on a chair facing her.

He took a deep breath.

"When I was sixteen I… I went a little wild once myself," he said, smiling faintly at the memory. "I filled my dad's pockets full of cotton wool balls."

Emma smiled; she'd never heard that story before and she could never have imagined her dad acting up and playing practical jokes, particularly on her grandfather!

They looked at each other for a moment and Emma could see the forgiveness in her father's eyes.

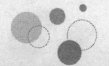
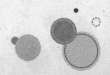

118

Maybe everything is *going to be okay*, she thought, trying to put the previous night behind her.

"So... your night was okay at least?" Emma asked hopefully.

Mr Gilbert grinned as he thought of the party and everything that had happened.

"Was Cleo supposed to say that speech?" he asked, chuckling.

"*No*," Emma giggled, screwing up her face at the thought of what must've gone on. "She improvised."

They both laughed and the tension in the air evaporated.

"But I do remember *some* of what I wrote," she added. "The last part was..."

Emma thought for a second, struggling to recall what she'd written.

"Dad, you were there the first time I ever went swimming. I never told you how scared I was, but knowing you were there gave me confidence," said Emma, looking into her dad's

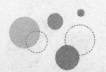
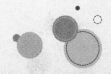

eyes. "You've always brought out the best in me, thank you."

Mr Gilbert felt his heart swell with pride.

"You're welcome," he said softly, touched by Emma's sincerity.

"I love you, dad," said Emma.

"I love you too, hon," Mr Gilbert replied, leaning forward to give Emma a big hug and a kiss.

I have the best family in the world, thought Emma happily, safe in the knowledge that whatever happened, they'd always be there to offer their support and unconditional love.

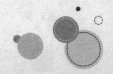

Chapter 12

Feeling like she needed to debrief with her friends after such an eventful night, Emma sent out a text message to Rikki, Cleo and Lewis to meet her down at the Juice-Net Café. When she arrived, she was comforted by the fact that spending the night there hadn't made it feel any different during the day – it was still the same old Juice-Net that she knew and loved – even if the pool table did make her feel a little sleepy every time she looked at it.

"I *never* want to go through another night like that," said Emma when the others arrived.

"Well neither do we, *believe me*," said Lewis, nudging Emma in the side to show that it was all over and there were no hard feelings.

"And the worst thing is… not knowing *exactly* what I did," she said, looking around at her friends.

"It's probably best you *don't* know," said

Rikki, rolling her eyes good-naturedly.

Emma sighed in resignation. She knew Rikki was right of course, but some part of her was intrigued. *How out-of-control was I?* she wondered to herself.

But in the end it didn't matter. Her friends had really rallied around her and kept her safe and she knew that was the main thing.

The four friends sat in silence, mulling over different events from the night before.

In fact they were all so lost in their own thoughts they didn't hear Byron come up behind them.

"Hey, Emma, thanks for last night," he said, placing his hands on her shoulders and smiling cheekily.

Emma turned, smiled back at him and was just about to say *You're very welcome*, when Byron quickly added, "I just wanted to say you've got the world's best lips."

Emma was so surprised she choked on her drink!

Rikki, Cleo and Lewis all stared straight

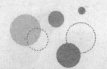
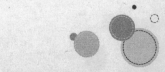

122

ahead, smirking delightedly at Emma's reaction.

Byron laughed too; he'd got the reaction he'd been looking for, and more.

"See ya," he said teasingly, smiling at them all and giving Emma a special wink before going off to join his friends at a table.

"Lips?" Emma shrieked once he'd gone. "*My* lips? What's he *talking* about?" Emma demanded, looking around the table with a mixture of surprise and glee.

The others looked at each and smiled knowingly.

"Guys? *Guys*?" Emma said insistently.

Seeing that they obviously weren't about to give anything away, Emma smiled and then shrugged.

It's true she couldn't remember the party, but perhaps the night hadn't been a *complete* disaster.

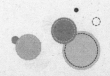

123